ALICE MUory
collections su
prizes and awards, including the International
Man Booker Prize, the National Book Critics Circle
Award and the Governor General's Award. She was
awarded the 2013 Nobel Prize for Literature.

'She has taken an art form, the short story ... and
she has cultivated it almost to perfection'
Peter Englund, Nobel Committee for Literature

'A true master of the form' Salman Rushdie

'Munro has ... concentrated upon provincial,
even back country lives, in tales of domestic
tragicomedy that seemed to open up, as if by
magic, into wider, deeper, vaster dimensions'
Joyce Carol Oates

'Alice Munro has a strong claim to being the best
fiction writer now working in North America'
Jonathan Franzen

'Among the major writers of English fiction of our
time' Margaret Atwood

'Read not more than one of her stories a day, and allow them to work their spell slowly: they are made to last' *Observer*

'She writes with a beautiful, mathematical clarity, an elemental humanity and a marvellous, limpid, funny apprehension of what goes on' *Sunday Telegraph*

'Some of the most honest, intuitive and exacting fiction, long or short, of our time' *The Times*

'Munro changed our sense of what the short story can do as radically as Chekhov ... she penetrates in words into the hidden roots of how we choose to live, and why we act' *New Yorker*

'One of the great short story writers not just of our time but of any time' *New York Times Book Review*

QUEENIE

A STORY BY

ALICE MUNRO

P

PROFILE BOOKS

This edition first published 2013

First published in book form in Great Britain in 1999 by
PROFILE BOOKS LTD
3A Exmouth House
Pine Street
London EC1R 0JH

Previously published in 1998 by
LONDON REVIEW OF BOOKS
28 Little Russell Street
London WC1A 2HN

Typeset in Quadraat
Designed by Peter Campbell
Printed and bound by CPI Group (UK) Ltd, Croydon, CR0 4YY

A CIP catalogue record for this book is available
from the British Library.

ISBN 978 1 78125 317 5

QUEENIE

QUEENIE said, 'Maybe you better stop calling me that,' and I said, 'What?'

'Stan doesn't like it,' she said. 'Queenie.'

It was a worse surprise to me to hear her say 'Stan' than to have her tell me to call her by her right name, which was Lena. But I could hardly expect her to go on calling him Mr Vorguilla, now that they were married, and had been for nearly two years. During that time I hadn't seen her, and for a moment when I saw her in the group of people waiting for the train at Union Station, I hadn't recognised her. Her hair was dyed black, and puffed up around her face in whatever style it was that in those days succeeded the beehive. Its beautiful corn-syrup colour – gold on top and dark underneath – as well as its silky length, was for ever lost. She wore a yellow print dress that skimmed her body and ended inches above her knees. The Cleopatra lines drawn heavily around her eyes, and the purply shadow, made her eyes seem smaller, not larger, as if they were deliberately hiding. She had pierced ears now, gold hoops swinging from them.

I hadn't known what to say to her. I saw her look at me with some surprise as well. I tried to be bold and easy-going. I said, 'Is that a dress or a frill around your bum?' She laughed, and I said, 'Was it ever hot on the train, I'm sweating like a pig.' I could hear my own loud voice, as twangy and vulgar as Bet's. Sweating like a pig.

Now on the streetcar going to Lena's place I couldn't stop the stupidity. I said, 'Are we still downtown?' The high buildings had been quickly left behind but I didn't think you could call this area residential. The same thing went on over and over again – a dry cleaner, a florist, a grocery store, a restaurant. Boxes of fruit and vegetables out on the sidewalk, signs for dentists and dressmakers and plumbing suppliers in the second-storey windows. Hardly a building higher than that, hardly a tree.

'It's not the real downtown,' said Queenie. 'Remember I showed you where Simpson's was? Where we got on the streetcar? That's the real.'

'So are we nearly there?' I said.

She said, 'We got a ways to go yet.' Then she

said, 'Way. Stan doesn't like me saying "ways" either.'

The repetition of things, or maybe the heat, was making me feel anxious and slightly sick. We were holding my suitcase on our knees and only a couple of inches ahead of my fingers was a man's fat neck and bald head. Just a few black, rather long hairs grew out of his head here and there, and they made me feel like throwing up. For some reason I thought of Mr Vorguilla's teeth in the medicine cabinet. Two teeth sitting beside his razor and shaving-brush and the wooden bowl holding his possibly hairy and disgusting shaving-soap. I had looked in the medicine cabinet when it wasn't any of my business and I brought Queenie in and showed her.

'I know,' she said. 'It's his bridge.'

'Why isn't he wearing them?'

'He is. He's wearing his others. These are his spares.'

'Yuck,' I said. 'Aren't they yellow?'

'Shut up,' said Queenie. But she was laughing.

Mrs Vorguilla was lying on the dining-room couch with her eyes shut, but maybe not sleeping.

'What he doesn't like about Queenie,' Queenie said, 'is he says it reminds him of a horse.'

*

When we got off the streetcar at last we had to walk up a steep hill, trying awkwardly to share the weight of the suitcase. The houses were not quite all the same though at first they looked like it. Some of the roofs came down over the walls like caps, or else the whole second storey was like a roof, covered in shingles. The shingles were dark green or maroon or brown. The porches came to within a few feet of the sidewalk and the spaces between the houses seemed narrow enough for people to reach out the side windows and shake hands. Children were playing on the sidewalk, but Queenie took no more notice of them than if they were birds pecking in the cracks. A very fat man, naked from the waist up, sat on his front staring at us in such a fixed and gloomy way that I was sure he had something to say to us. But Queenie marched on past him.

She turned in partway up the hill, following a

gravel path between some garbage tins. Out of an upstairs window a woman called something that I found unintelligible. Queenie called back, 'It's just my sister, she's visiting.'

'Our landlady,' she said. 'They live in the front and upstairs. They're Greeks. She doesn't speak hardly any English.'

It turned out that Queenie and Mr Vorguilla shared a bathroom with the Greeks. You took your roll of toilet paper with you – if you forgot, there wasn't any. I had to go in there at once, because I was menstruating heavily and had to change my pad. For years afterwards, the sight of certain city streets on hot days, certain shades of brown brick and dark-painted shingles, and the noise of streetcars, would bring back to me the memory of cramps low in the belly, waves of flushing, bodily leakage and confusion.

There was one bedroom where Queenie slept with Mr Vorguilla, and another bedroom turned into a small living-room, and a narrow kitchen, and a sun porch. The cot in the sun porch was where I was to sleep. Close outside the windows the landlord and another man were fixing a motorcycle. The smell of oil, of metal and machinery mixed with the smell of ripe tomatoes in the sun. There was a radio blaring music out of an upstairs window.

'One thing Stan can't stand,' said Queenie. 'That radio.' She pulled the flowered curtains close, but the noise and sun still came through. 'I wish I could've afforded lining,' she said.

I had the old pad wrapped up in toilet paper, in my hand. She brought me a paper bag and directed me to the outdoor garbage pail. 'Every one of them,' she said. 'Out there right away. You won't forget, will you?'

I still tried to be nonchalant, and act as if I felt welcome. 'I need to get a nice cool dress like yours,' I said.

'Maybe I could make you one,' said Queenie, with her head in the fridge. 'I want a Coke, do you? I just go to this place they sell remnants. I made this whole dress for around three dollars. What size are you now, anyway?'

'Fourteen,' I said. 'But I'm trying to lose.'

'Still. We could maybe find something.'

*

'I am going to marry a lady that has a little girl about your age,' my father had said. 'And this little girl has not got any father. So you have to promise me one thing and that is that you will never tease her or say anything mean to her about that. There'll be times when you may get in a fight and disagree with each other the way sisters do but that is one thing you never must say. And if other kids say it you never take their side.'

For the sake of argument, I said that I did not have a mother and nobody said anything mean to me.

My father said, 'That's different.'

He was wrong about everything. We did not seem anywhere near the same age, because Queenie was nine, when my father married Bet, and I was six. Though later, after I had skipped a grade and Queenie had failed one, we came closer together in school. And I never knew anyone to try to be mean to Queenie. She was somebody everybody wanted to be friends with. She was chosen first for a baseball team even though she was a careless baseball player, and first for a spelling team though she was a poor speller. Also, she and

I did not get into fights. Not once. She showed plenty of kindness towards me and I had plenty of admiration for her. I would have worshipped her for her dark-gold hair and her sleepy-looking dark eyes and her giggly easy-going confidence, even if she had not been kind. But for a pretty girl she had an extraordinarily sweet nature.

*

As soon as I woke up on the morning of Queenie's disappearance, that morning in early winter, I felt her absence.

It was still dark, between six and seven o'clock. The house was cold. I pulled on the big woolly brown bathrobe that Queenie and I shared. We called it Buffalo Bill and whichever of us got out of bed first in the morning would grab it. A mystery where it came from. 'Maybe a friend of Bet's before she married your Dad,' Queenie said. 'But don't say anything, she'd kill me.'

Her bed was empty and she wasn't in the bathroom. I went down the stairs not turning any lights on, not wanting to wake Bet. I looked out the little

14

window in the front door. The hard pavement, the sidewalk, and the flat grass in the front yard all glittering with frost. The snow was late. I turned up the hall thermostat and the furnace rolled over in the dark, gave its reliable growl. We had just got the oil furnace and my father said he still woke up at five every morning, thinking it was time to go down to the cellar and build up the fire.

My father slept in what had been a pantry, off the kitchen. He had an iron bed and a broken-backed chair he kept his stack of old *National Geographics* on, to read when he couldn't sleep. He turned the ceiling light off and on by a cord tied to the bedframe. This whole arrangement seemed to me quite natural and proper for the man of the house, the father. He should sleep like a sentry with a coarse blanket for cover and an unhousebroken smell about him, of engines and tobacco. Reading and wakeful till all hours and alert all through his sleep.

Even so, he hadn't heard Queenie. He said she must be somewhere in the house. 'Did you look in the bathroom?'

I said, 'She's not there.'

'Maybe in with her mother. Case of the heebie-jeebies.'

My father called it the heebie-jeebies when Bet woke up – or didn't quite wake up – from a bad dream. She would come blundering out of her room unable to say what had frightened her, and Queenie had to be the one to guide her back to bed. Queenie would curl against her back making comforting noises like a puppy lapping milk, and Bet would not remember anything in the morning.

I had turned the kitchen light on.

'I didn't want to wake her,' I said. 'Bet.'

I looked at the rusty-bottomed bread tin swiped too often by the dishcloth, and the pots sitting on the stove, washed but not put away, and the motto supplied by Fairholme Dairy: The Lord is the Heart of Our House. All these things stupidly waiting for the day to begin and not knowing that it had been hollowed out by catastrophe.

The door to the side porch had been unlocked.

'Somebody came in,' I said. 'Somebody came in and took Queenie.'

My father came out with his trousers on over his long underwear. Bet was slapping downstairs in her slippers and her chenille robe, flicking on lights as she came.

'Queenie not in with you?' my father said. To me he said, 'The door had to've been unlocked from the inside.'

Bet said, 'What's this about Queenie?'

'She might just have felt like a walk,' my father said.

Bet ignored this. She had a mask of some pink stuff dried on her face. She never sold any cosmetic she had not tried on herself.

'You get over to Vorguilla's,' she said to me. 'She might've thought of something she was supposed to do over there.'

This was a week or so after Mrs Vorguilla's funeral, but Queenie had kept on working there, helping to box up dishes and linens so that Mr Vorguilla could move into an apartment. He had the Christmas concerts to get ready for and could not do all the packing himself. Bet wanted Queenie to just quit, so that she could get taken on for Christmas help at one of the stores.

I put on my father's rubber boots that were by the door, instead of going upstairs for my shoes. I stumbled across the yard to the Vorguillas' porch and rang the bell. It was a chime that seemed to proclaim the musicality of the household. I hugged Buffalo Bill tight around me and prayed. Oh, Queenie, Queenie, turn the lights on. I forgot that if Queenie was working in there, the lights would be on already.

No answer. I pounded on the wood. Mr Vorguilla was going to be in a bad temper when I finally woke him. I pressed my head to the door, listening for stirrings.

'Mr Vorguilla. Mr Vorguilla. I'm sorry to wake you, Mr Vorguilla. Is anybody home?'

A window was heaved up in the house on the other side of the Vorguillas'. Mr Hovey, an old bachelor, lived there with his sister.

'Use your eyes,' Mr Hovey called down. 'Look in the driveway.'

Mr Vorguilla's car was gone.

Mr Hovey slammed down the window.

When I opened our kitchen door I saw my father and Bet sitting at the table with cups of tea in front of them. For a minute I thought that order had been restored. There had been a phone call, perhaps, with some pacifying news.

'Mr Vorguilla isn't there,' I said. 'His car's gone.'

'Oh, we know that,' Bet said. 'We know all about that.'

My father said, 'Look at here,' and pushed a piece of paper across the table.

'I am going to marry Mr Vorguilla,' it said. 'Yours truly, Queenie.'

'Underneath the sugar bowl,' said my father.

Bet dropped her spoon.

'I want him prosecuted,' she shouted. 'I want her in reform school. I want the police.'

My father said, 'She's 18 years old and she can get married if she wants to. The police aren't going to set up a road-block.'

'Who says they're on the road? They're shacked up in some motel. That fool of a girl and that bug-eyed pickle-ass.'

'Talk like that isn't going to bring her back.'

'I don't want her back. Not if she comes crawling. She's made her bed and she can lie in it, with her bug-eyed bugger. He can screw her in the ear for all I care.'

My father said, 'That's enough.'

Queenie brought me a couple of 222s to take with my Coke. 'It's amazing how your cramps clear up,' she said. 'It's a benefit of being married.'

'Your Dad went and told you,' she said. 'He told you about us.'

When I told my father I wanted to get a summer job, before entering Teachers' College in the fall, he had said that maybe I should go to Toronto and look up Queenie. He told me that she had written to him in care of his trucking business, asking if he could let them have some money to tide them over the winter.

'I would've never had to write to him,' Queenie said, 'if Stan hadn't got sick last year with pneumonia.'

I said, 'It was the first I knew where you were.' Tears came into my eyes, I didn't know why. Because I'd felt so happy when I found out, so lonely before I found out, because I wished right now that she would say, 'Of course, I always meant to get in touch with you,' and she didn't say it.

'Bet doesn't know,' I said. 'She thinks I'm on my own.'

'I hope not,' Queenie said. 'I mean I hope she doesn't know.'

I had a lot of things to tell her, about home. I told her that the trucking firm had gone from three vehicles to a dozen, and that Bet had bought a muskrat coat and expanded her business, holding Beauty Clinics now in our house. She had fixed over the room where my father used to sleep for these purposes, and he had moved his cot and the *National Geographics* to his office – an air force billet he had towed to the trucking yard. Sitting at the kitchen table studying for my Senior Matric I had listened to Bet say, 'A skin this delicate, you should never go near it with a washcloth,' prior to loading up some raw-faced woman with lotions and creams. And sometimes in a no less intense, but less hopeful tone, 'I'm telling you I had Evil, I had Evil living right next door to me and I never suspected it, because you don't, do you? I always think the best of people. Right up till they kick me between the eyes.'

Never the words 'bugger', 'screwed', 'greasy-prick', used in private.

'That's right,' the customer would say. 'I'm the same.'

Or, 'You think you know what sorrow is, but you don't know half.'

Then she'd come back from seeing the woman to the door and say, 'Touch her face in the dark and you'd never know the difference from sandpaper, what can I do?'

Queenie didn't seem interested in hearing about these things. And there was not much time anyway. Before we had finished our Cokes there were quick hard steps on the gravel and Mr Vorguilla came into the kitchen.

'So look who's here,' cried Queenie. She half got up, as if to touch him, but he veered toward the sink.

Her voice was full of such laughing surprise that I wondered if he had been told anything about my letter or the fact that I was on my way.

'It's Chrissy,' she said.

'So I see,' said Mr Vorguilla. 'You must like hot weather, Chrissy, if you come to Toronto in the summer.'

'She's going to look for a job,' said Queenie.

'And do you have some qualifications,' Mr Vorguilla said. 'Do you have qualifications for finding a job in Toronto?'

Queenie said, 'She's got her Senior Matric.'

'Well let's hope that's good enough,' said Mr Vorguilla. He ran a glass of water and drank it all down, standing with his back to us. Exactly as he used to do when Mrs Vorguilla and Queenie and I were sitting at the kitchen table in that other house, the Vorguillas' house next door. Mr Vorguilla would come in from a practice somewhere, or he would be taking a break from teaching a piano lesson in the front room. At the sound of his steps Mrs Vorguilla would have given up a warning smile. And we all looked down at our Scrabble letters, giving him the option of noticing us or not. Sometimes he didn't. The opening of the cupboard, the turning of the tap, the setting of the glass down on the counter, were like a series of little explosions. As if he dared anybody to breathe while he was there.

When he taught us music at school he was just the same. He came into the classroom with the step of a man who had not a minute to lose and he rapped the pointer once and it was time to start. Up and down the aisles he strutted with his ears cocked, his bulgy blue eyes alert, his expression tense and quarrel-some. At any moment he might stop by your desk to listen to your singing, to see if you were faking or out of tune. Then he'd bring his head slowly down, his eyes bulging into yours and his hands working to shush the other voices, to bring you to your shame. And the word was that he was just as much a dicta-tor with his various choirs and glee clubs. Yet he was a favourite with his singers, particularly with ladies. They knitted him things at Christmas. Socks and mufflers and mitts to keep him warm on his trips between school and school and choir and choir.

When Queenie had the run of the house, after Mrs Vorguilla got too sick to manage, she fished out of a drawer a knitted object that she flapped in front of my face. It had arrived without the name of its donor.

'It's a peter-heater,' Queenie said. 'Mrs Vorguilla said don't show it to him, he would just get mad. Don't you know what a peter-heater is?'

I said, 'Ugh.'

'It's just a joke,' she said.

*

Both Queenie and Mr Vorguilla had to go out to work in the evenings. Mr Vorguilla played the piano in a restaurant. He wore a tuxedo. And Queenie had a job selling tickets in a movie theatre. The theatre was just a few blocks away, so I walked there with her. And when I saw her sitting in the ticket-booth I understood that the make-up and the dyed puffed hair and the hoop earrings were not so strange after all. Queenie looked like some of the girls passing on the street or going in to see the movie with their boyfriends. And she looked very much like some of the girls portrayed in the posters that surrounded her. She looked to be connected to the world of drama, of heated love affairs and dangers, that was being depicted inside on the screen.

She looked – in my father's words – as if she didn't have to take a back seat to anybody.

'Why don't you just wander around for a while?' she had said to me. But I felt conspicuous. I couldn't imagine sitting in a café drinking coffee and advertising to the world that I had nothing to do and no place to go. Or going into a store and trying on clothes that I had no hope of buying. I climbed the hill again, I waved hello to the Greek woman calling out her window. I let myself in with Queenie's key.

I sat on the cot in the sun porch. There was nowhere to hang up the clothes I had brought and I thought it might not be such a good idea to unpack, anyway. Mr Vorguilla might not like to see any sign that I was staying.

I thought that Mr Vorguilla's looks had changed, just as Queenie's had. But his had not changed, as hers had, in the direction of what seemed to me a hard foreign glamour and sophistication. His hair, which had been reddish-grey, was now quite grey, and the expression of his face – always ready to flash with outrage at the possibility of disrespect or an inadequate performance or just at the fact of something in his house not being where it was supposed to be – seemed now to be one of more permanent grievance, as if some insult was being offered or bad behaviour going unpunished, all the time in front of his eyes.

I got up and walked around the apartment. You

can never get a good look at the places people live in while they are there.

The kitchen was the nicest room, though too dark. Queenie had ivy growing up around the window over the sink, and she had wooden spoons sticking up out of a pretty, handleless mug, just the way Mrs Vorguilla used to have them. The living-room had the piano in it, the same piano that had been in the other living-room. There was one armchair and a bookshelf made with bricks and planks and a record-player and a lot of records sitting on the floor. No television. No walnut rocking-chairs or tapestry curtains. Not even the floor-lamp with the Japanese scenes on its parchment shade. Yet all these things had been moved to Toronto, on a snowy day. I had been home at lunchtime and had seen the moving-truck. Bet couldn't move from the front door. Finally she forgot all the dignity she usually liked to show to strangers and opened the door and yelled at the moving-men, 'You go back to Toronto and tell him if he ever shows his face around here again he'll wish he hadn't.'

The moving-men waved cheerfully as if they were used to scenes like this and maybe they were.

Moving furniture must expose you to a lot of ranting and raging.

But where had everything gone? Sold, I thought. It must have been sold. My father had said that it sounded as if Mr Vorguilla was having a hard time getting going down in Toronto, in his line of work. And Queenie had said something about 'getting behind'. She would never have written to my father if they hadn't gotten behind.

They must have sold the furniture before she wrote.

On the bookshelf I saw *The Encyclopedia of Music*, and *The World Companion to Opera*, and *The Lives of the Great Composers*. Also the large thin book with the beautiful cover – the *Rubáiyát of Omar Khayyam* – that Mrs Vorguilla often had beside her couch.

There was another book with a similarly decorated cover whose exact title I don't remember. Something in the title made me think I might like it. The word 'flowered' or 'perfumed'. I opened it up and I can remember well enough the sentence I read.

'The young odalisques in the harim were also instructed in the exquisite use of their fingernails.'

Something close to that, at any rate.

I was not sure what an odalisque was, but the word 'harim' (why not 'harem') gave me a clue. And I had to read on, to find out what they were taught to do with their fingernails. I read on and on, maybe for an hour, and then let the book fall to the floor. I had feelings of excitement, and disgust, and disbelief. Was this the sort of thing that really grown-up people took an interest in? Even the design on the cover, the pretty vines all curved and twisted, seemed slightly hostile and mocking. I picked the book up to put it back in its place and it fell open to show the names on the fly-leaf. Stan and Marigold Vorguilla. In a feminine handwriting. Stan and Marigold.

I thought of Mrs Vorguilla's high white forehead and tight little grey-black curls. Her pearl-button earrings and blouses that tied with a bow at the neck. She was taller by quite a bit than Mr Vorguilla and people thought that was why they did not go out together. But it was really because she got out of breath. She got out of breath walking upstairs, or hanging the clothes on the line. And finally she got out of breath even sitting at the table playing Scrabble.

At first my father would not let us take any money for fetching her groceries or hanging up her washing – he said it was only neighbourly.

Bet said she thought she would try laying around and see if people would come and wait on her for nothing.

Then Mr Vorguilla came over and negotiated for Queenie to go and work for them. Queenie wanted to go because she had failed her year at high school and didn't want to repeat it. At last Bet said all right, but told her she was not to do any nursing.

'If he's too cheap to hire a nurse that's not your lookout.'

Queenie said that Mr Vorguilla put out the pills every morning and gave Mrs Vorguilla a sponge-bath every evening. He even tried to wash her sheets in the bathtub as if there was not such a thing as a washing-machine in the house.

I thought of the times when we would be playing Scrabble in the kitchen and Mr Vorguilla after drinking his glass of water would put a hand on Mrs Vorguilla's shoulder and sigh, as if he had come back from a long wearying journey.

'Hello pet,' he would say.

Mrs Vorguilla would duck her head to give his hand a dry kiss.

'Hello pet,' she would say.

Then he would look at us, at Queenie and me, as if our presence did not absolutely offend him.

'Hello you two.'

Later on Queenie and I would giggle in our beds in the dark.

'Goodnight pet.'

'Goodnight pet.'

I wished that we could go back to that time.

★

Except for going to the bathroom in the morning and sneaking out to put my pad in the garbage pail, I sat on my made-up cot in the sun porch until Mr Vorguilla was out of the house. I was afraid he might not have any place to go but apparently he did. As soon as he was gone Queenie called to me. She had set out a peeled orange and cornflakes and coffee.

'And here's the paper,' she said. 'I was looking at

the Help Wanteds. First though I want to do something with your hair. I want to cut some off the back
and I want to do it up in rollers, okay with you?'

I said okay. Even while I was eating Queenie kept
circling me and looking at me, trying to work out
her idea. Then she got me up on a stool – I was still
drinking my coffee – and she began to comb and
snip.

'What kind of a job are we looking for, now?' she
said. 'I saw one at a dry cleaners. At the counter.
How would that be?'

I said, 'That'd be fine.'

'Are you still planning on being a school-
teacher?' she said.

I said I didn't know. I had an idea that she might
think that a drab sort of occupation.

'I think you should be. You're smart enough.
Teachers get paid more. They get paid more than
people like me. You've got more independence.'

But it was all right, she said, working at the
movie theatre. She had got the job a month or so
before last Christmas and she was really happy
then because she had her own money at last and
could buy the ingredients for a Christmas cake.

And she became friends with a man who was selling Christmas trees off the back of a truck. He let her have one for fifty cents, and she hauled it up the hill herself. She hung streamers of red and green crêpe paper, which was cheap. She made some ornaments out of silver foil on cardboard and bought others on the day before Christmas when they went on sale in the drugstore. She made cookies and hung them on the tree as she had seen in a magazine. It was a European custom.

She wanted to have a party but she didn't know who to ask. There were the Greek people, and Stan had a couple of friends. Then she got the idea of asking his students.

I still couldn't get used to her saying 'Stan'. It wasn't just the reminder of her intimacy with Mr Vorguilla. It was that, of course. But it was also the feeling it gave, that she had made him up from scratch. A new person. Stan. As if there had never been a Mr Vorguilla, that we had known together – let alone a Mrs Vorguilla – in the first place.

Stan's students were all adults by that time – he really preferred adults to schoolchildren – so they didn't have to worry about the sort of games and entertainment you plan for children. They held the party on a Sunday evening, because all the other evenings were taken up with Stan's work at the restaurant and Queenie's at the theatre.

The Greeks brought wine they had made and some of the students brought eggnog mix and rum and sherry. And some brought records you could dance to. They had thought that Stan wouldn't have any records of that kind of music and they were right.

Queenie made sausage-rolls and gingerbread and the Greek woman brought her own kind of cookies. Everything was good. The party was a success. Queenie danced with a Chinese boy named Andrew, who had brought a record she loved.

'Turn, turn, turn,' she said, and I moved my head as directed. She laughed and said, 'No, no, I didn't mean you. That's the record. That's the song. It's by the Byrds.'

'Turn, turn, turn,' she sang. 'To everything, there is a season –'

Andrew was a dentistry student. But he wanted to learn to play the Moonlight Sonata. Stan said that was going to take him a long time. Andrew was patient. He told Queenie that he could not afford to go home for Christmas. His home was in Northern Ontario.

'I thought he was from China,' I said.

'No, not Chinese Chinese. From here.'

They did play one children's game. They played musical chairs. Everybody was boisterous by that time. Even Stan. He pulled Queenie down into his lap when she was running past, and he wouldn't let her go. And then when everybody had gone he wouldn't let her clean up. He just wanted her to come to bed.

'You know the way men are,' Queenie said. 'Do you have a boyfriend yet, or anything?'

I said no. The last man my father had hired as a driver was always coming to the house to deliver some unimportant message, and my father said, 'He just wants a chance to talk to Chrissy.' I was cool to him, however, and so far he hadn't got up the nerve to ask me out. I didn't want to go out with anybody from home.

'So you don't really know about that stuff yet?' said Queenie.

I said, 'Of course I know.'

'You don't sound like you do,' she said.

The guests at the party had eaten up nearly everything but the cake. They did not eat much of that but Queenie wasn't offended. It was very rich, and by the time they got to it they were filled up with sausage-rolls and other things. Also, it had not had time to ripen the way the book said it should, so she was just as glad to have some left over. She was thinking, before Stan pulled her away, that she should get the cake wrapped up in a wine-soaked cloth and put it in a cool place. She was either thinking of doing that or she had actually done it, and in the morning she saw that the cake was not on the table so she thought she had done it. She thought good, the cake was put away.

A day or so later Stan said, 'Let's have a piece of that cake.' She said oh, let it ripen a bit more, but he insisted. She went to the cupboard and then to the refrigerator, but it was not there. She looked high and low and she could not find it. She thought back to seeing it on the table. And a memory came to her, of getting a clean cloth and soaking it in wine and wrapping that carefully around the leftover cake. And then of wrapping waxed paper around the outside of the cloth. But when had she done that? Had she done it at all or only dreamed about it? Where had she put the cake when she finished wrapping it? She tried to see herself putting it away but her mind went blank.

She looked all through the cupboard, but she knew the cake was too big to be hidden there. Then she looked in the oven and even in insane places like her dresser drawers and under the bed and on the closet shelf. It was nowhere.

'If you put it somewhere, then it must be somewhere,' Stan said.

'I did. I put it somewhere,' said Queenie.

'Maybe you were drunk and you threw it out.'

She said, 'I wasn't drunk. I didn't throw it out.'

But she went and looked in the garbage. No.

He sat at the table watching her. If you put it somewhere it must be somewhere. She was getting frantic.

'Are you sure?' said Stan. 'Are you sure you didn't just give it away?'

She was sure. She was sure she hadn't given it away. She had wrapped it up to keep. She was sure, she was almost sure she had wrapped it to keep. She was sure she had not given it away.

'Oh, I don't know about that,' Stan said. 'I think maybe you gave it away. And I think I know who to.'

Queenie was brought to a standstill. Who to?

'I think you gave it to Andrew.'

To Andrew?

Oh yes. Poor Andrew who was telling her he couldn't afford to go home for Christmas. She was sorry for Andrew.

'So you gave him our cake.'

No, said Queenie. Why would she do that? She would not do that. She had never thought of giving Andrew the cake.

Stan said, 'Lena. Don't lie.'

That was the beginning of Queenie's long miserable struggle. All she could say was no. No, no, I did not give the cake to anybody. I did not give the cake to Andrew. I am not lying. No. No.

'Probably you were drunk,' Stan said. 'You were drunk and you are not remembering very well.'

Queenie said she was not drunk.

'You were the one who was drunk,' she said.

He got up and came at her with his hand raised,

saying not to tell him that he'd been drunk, never to tell him that.

Queenie cried out, 'I won't. I won't. I'm sorry.' And he didn't hit her. But she began to cry. She kept crying while she tried to persuade him. Why would she give away the cake she had worked so hard to make? Why would he not believe her? Why would she lie to him?

'Everybody lies,' Stan said. And the more she cried and begged him to believe her, the more cool and sarcastic he became.

'Use a little logic,' he said. 'If it's here, get up and find it. If it isn't here, then you gave it away.'

Queenie said that wasn't logic. It did not have to be given away, just because she could not find it. Then he came close to her again in such a calm half-smiling way that she thought for a moment he was going to kiss her. Instead he closed his hands around her throat and just for a second cut off her breath. He didn't even leave any marks.

'Now,' he said. 'Now – are you going to teach me about logic?'

Then he went to get dressed to go and play at the restaurant.

He stopped speaking to her. He wrote her a note saying he would speak to her again when she told the truth. All over Christmas she could not stop crying. She and Stan were supposed to go and visit the Greek people on Christmas day but she couldn't go, her face was such a mess. Stan had to go and say that she was sick. The Greek people probably knew the truth anyway. They had probably heard the hullabaloo through the walls.

She put on a ton of make-up and went to work and the manager said, 'You want to give the people the idea this is a tragedy?' She said she had infected sinuses and he let her go home.

When Stan came home that night and pretended she didn't exist she turned over and looked at him. She knew that he would get into bed and lie beside her like a post and that if she moved against him he would continue to lie like a post until she moved away. She saw that he could go on living like this and she could not. She thought that if she had to go on in this way she would die. Just as if he really had choked off her breath, she would die.

So she said, forgive me.

Forgive me. I did what you said. I'm sorry.

Please. Please. I'm sorry.

He sat down on the bed. He didn't say anything.

She said that she had really forgotten about giving the cake away but that now she remembered that she had done it and she was sorry.

'I wasn't lying,' she said. 'I forgot.'

'You forgot you gave the cake to Andrew?' he said.

'I must have. I forgot.'

'To Andrew. You gave it to Andrew.'

Yes, Queenie said. Yes, yes, that was what she had done. And she began to howl and hang on to him and beg him to forgive her.

All right, stop the hysterics, he said. He did not say that he forgave her but he got a warm washcloth and wiped her face and lay down beside her and cuddled her and pretty soon he wanted to do everything else.

'No more music lessons for Mr Moonlight Sonata,' he finally said.

What a relief.

And then to top it all off, later she found the cake.

She found it wrapped up in a dishtowel and then

wrapped in waxed paper just as she had remembered. And put into a shopping bag and hung from a hook in the back porch. Of course. The sun porch was the ideal place because it got too cold to use in winter, but it wasn't freezing cold. She must have been thinking that when she hung the cake there. That this was the ideal place. And then she forgot. She was a little drunk – she had to be. She had forgotten absolutely. And there it was.

She found it, and she threw it all out. She never told Stan.

'I pitched it,' she said.' It was just as good as ever and all that expensive fruit and stuff in it but there was no way I wanted to get that subject brought up again. So I just pitched it out.'

Her voice which had been so woeful in the bad parts of the story was now sly and full of laughter, as if all the time she had been telling me a joke, and throwing out the cake was the final, ridiculous point of it.

I had to pull my head out of her hands and turn around and look at her.

I said, 'But he was wrong.'

'Well of course he was *wrong*,' she said. 'Men are

not *normal*, Chrissy. That's one thing you'll learn if you ever get married.'

'I never will then,' I said. 'I never will get married.'

'He was just jealous,' she said. 'He was just so jealous.'

'Never,' I said.

'Well you and me are very different, Chrissy. Very different.' She sighed. She said, 'I am a creature of love.'

I thought that you might see these words on a movie poster. A creature of love. Maybe on a poster of one of the movies that had played at Queenie's theatre.

'You are going to look so good when I take these rollers out,' she said. 'You won't be saying you haven't got a boyfriend for very long.'

'But it'll be too late to go looking today,' she said. 'Early bird tomorrow. If Stan asks you anything say you went to a couple of places and they took your phone number. Say a store or a restaurant or anything just so long as he thinks you're looking.'

I was hired the next day at the first place I tried, though I hadn't managed to be such an early bird after all. Queenie had decided to do my hair still another way and to make up my eyes, but the result was not what she had hoped for. 'You're really more the natural type after all,' she said, and I scrubbed it all off and put on my own red lipstick.

By this time it was too late for Queenie to go out with me, to check on her Post Office box. She had to get ready to go to the movie theatre. It was a Saturday, so she had to work in the afternoon as well as in the evening. She got out her key and asked me to check the box for her, as a favour. She explained to me where it was.

'I had to get my own box when I wrote to your Dad,' she said.

*

The job I got was in a drugstore in the basement of an apartment building. I was hired to work behind the lunch counter. When I first came in I felt fairly hopeless. My hairstyle was drooping in the heat and I had a moustache of sweat on my upper lip. At least my cramps had moderated.

A woman in a white uniform was at the counter, drinking coffee.

'Did you come about the job?' she said.

I said yes. The woman had a hard square face, pencilled eyebrows, a beehive of purplish hair.

'You speak English, do you?'

'Yes.'

'I mean you didn't just learn it? You're not a foreigner?'

I said I wasn't.

'I tried out two girls in the last two days and I had to let them both go. One let on she could speak English but she couldn't and the other I had to tell her everything ten times over. Wash your hands good at the sink and I'll get you an apron. My husband is the pharmacist and I do the till.' (I noticed for the first time a grey-haired man behind a high counter in the corner, looking at me and pretending not to.) 'It's slow now but it'll get busy in a while. It's all old people in this block and after their naps they start coming down here wanting coffee.'

I tied on an apron and took my place behind the counter. Hired for a job in Toronto. I tried to find out where things were without asking questions and had to ask only two – how to work the coffee-maker and what to do about the money.

'You make out the bill and they bring it to me. What did you think?'

It was all right. People came in one or two at a time mostly wanted coffee or a Coke. I kept the cups washed and wiped the counter clean and apparently I made out the bills properly as there was no complaint. The customers were mostly old people as the woman had said. Some spoke to me in a kindly way, saying I was new here and even asking where I came from. Others seemed to be in a kind of trance. One woman wanted toast and I managed that. Then I did a ham sandwich. There was a little flurry with four people there at once. A man wanted pie and ice-cream and I found the ice-cream hard as cement to scoop out. But I did it. I got more confident. I said to them. 'Here you are,' when I set down their orders, and 'Here's the damage,' when I presented the bill.

In a slow moment the woman from the till came over.

'I see you made somebody toast,' she said. 'Can you read?'

She pointed to a sign stuck on the mirror behind the counter.

NO BREAKFAST ITEMS
SERVED AFTER 11 A.M.

I said that I thought it was okay to make toast, if you could make toasted sandwiches.

'Well you thought wrong. Toasted sandwiches yes, ten cents extra. Toast, no. Do you understand now?'

I said yes. I wasn't so crushed as I might have been at first. All the time I was working I thought what a relief it would be to go back and tell Mr Vorguilla that yes, I had a job. Now I could go and look for a room of my own to live in. Maybe tomorrow, Sunday, if the drugstore was closed. If I even had one room, I thought, Queenie would have some place to run away to if Mr Vorguilla got mad at her again. And if Queenie ever decided to leave Mr Vorguilla (I persisted in thinking of this as a possibility in spite of how Queenie had finished her story) then with the pay from both our jobs maybe we could get a little apartment. Or at least a room with a hotplate and a toilet and shower to ourselves. It would be like when we lived at home with our parents except that our parents would be away.

I garnished each sandwich with a bit of torn off lettuce and a dill pickle. That was what another sign on the mirror promised. But when I got the dill pickle out of a jar I thought it looked like too much so I cut it in half. I had just served a man a sandwich in this way when the woman from the till came over and got herself a cup of coffee. She took her coffee back to the till and drank it standing up. When the man had finished his sandwich and paid for it and left the store she came over again.

'You gave that man half a dill pickle. Have you been doing that with every sandwich?'

I said yes.

'Don't you know how to slice a pickle? One pickle ought to last ten sandwiches.'

I looked at the sign. I said, 'It doesn't say a slice. It says a pickle.'

'That's enough,' the woman said. 'Get out of that apron. I don't take any back talk from my employees, that's one thing I don't take. You can get your purse and get out of here. And don't go asking me where's your pay because you haven't been any use to me anyway and this was just supposed to be training.'

The grey-haired man was peeking out again, with a faint smile.

So I found myself out on the street again, walking to the streetcar stop. But I knew the way some streets went now and I knew how to use a transfer. I had even had experience at a job. I could say that I had worked behind a lunch counter. If anybody wanted a reference it would be tricky – but I could say the lunch counter was in my home town. While I waited for the streetcar I took out the list of other places where I meant to apply, and the map that Queenie had given me. But it was later than I'd thought and most places seemed too far away. I dreaded having to tell Mr Vorguilla. I decided to walk back, in the hopes that when I got there he'd have gone.

I had just turned up the hill when I remembered

the Post Office. I found my way back to it and got a letter out of the box and walked home again. Surely he would be gone by now, I thought.

But he wasn't. When I walked past the open living-room window that overlooked the path beside the house, I heard music. It wasn't what Queenie would play. It was the sort of complicated music that we had heard sometimes coming through the open windows of the Vorguillas' house – music that demanded your attention and then didn't go anywhere, or at least didn't go anywhere fast enough. Classical.

Queenie was in the kitchen, wearing another of her skimpy dresses, and all her make-up. She had bangles on her arms. She was setting tea-cups on a tray. I was dizzy for a moment, coming out of the sunlight, and every inch of my skin bloomed with sweat.

'Shh,' Queenie said, because I'd closed the door with a crash. 'They're in there listening to records. It's him and his friend Leslie.'

Just as she said this the music came to an abrupt halt and there was a burst of excited talk.

'One of them plays a record and the other has to

guess what it is just from a little bit of it,' Queenie said. 'They play these little bits and then stop, over and over. It drives you crazy.' She started cutting slices off a delicatessen chicken and putting them on buttered slices of bread. 'Did you get a job?' she said.

'Yes but it wasn't permanent.'

'Oh well.' She didn't seem very interested. But as the music started again she looked up and smiled and said, 'Did you go to the –' And she saw the letter I was carrying in my hand.

She dropped the knife and came to me in a hurry, saying softly. 'You walked right in with it in your hand, I should have told you, put it in your purse. My private letter.' She grabbed it from my hand and right at that moment the kettle on the stove began to shriek.

'Oh, get the kettle,' she said. 'Chrissy, quick, quick. Get the kettle or he'll be out here, he can't stand the sound.'

She had turned her back and was tearing open the envelope.

I took the kettle off the burner, and she said, 'Make the tea, please –' in the soft preoccupied voice of somebody reading an urgent message.

'Is it in the pot?' I said.

'Yes, yes, just pour the water on, it's measured.' She laughed as if my asking her that was a joke. I poured the water on the tea-leaves and she said, 'Thanks. Oh, thanks, Chrissy, thanks.' She turned around and looked at me. Her face was rosy and all the bangles on her arms jingled with a delicate agitation. She folded up the letter and pulled up her skirt and tucked it under the elastic waistband of her underpants.

She said, 'Sometimes he goes through my purse.'

I said, 'Is the tea for them?'

'Yes. And I have to get back to work. Oh, what am I doing? I have to cut the sandwiches. Where's the knife?'

I picked up the knife and cut the sandwiches and put them on a plate.

'Don't you want to know who my letter's from?' she said.

I couldn't think. I still had the sensation of the room moving around me, though it wasn't doing that any more in a physical way.

I said, 'Bet?'

Because I had a hope that a private forgiveness from Bet could be the thing that had made Queenie burst into flower.

I had not even looked at the writing on the envelope.

Queenie's face changed, her mouth curled, and she said, 'Hardly.' Then she recovered her happiness. She came and put her arms around me and spoke into my ear, in a voice that was shivering and shy and triumphant. 'It's from Andrew,' she said. 'Can you take the tray in to them. I can't. I can't right now. Oh, thank you.'

*

Before Queenie went off to work she came into the living-room and kissed both Mr Vorguilla and his friend. She kissed both of them on their foreheads. She gave me a butterfly wave and said, 'Bye bye.'

When I had brought the tray in I saw the annoyance on Mr Vorguilla's face, that it wasn't Queenie. But he spoke to me in a surprisingly tolerant way and introduced me to Leslie. Leslie was a stout bald man who at first looked to me almost as old as Mr Vorguilla, but when you got used to him and took his baldness into account he looked much younger. He was not the sort of friend I would have expected Mr Vorguilla to have. He was not brusque or know-it-all but comfortable and full of encouragement. For example, when I told about my employment at the lunch counter he said, 'Well you know that's something. Getting hired the first place you tried. It shows you know how to make a good impression.'

I had not found the experience hard to talk about. The presence of Leslie made everything easier and seemed to soften the behaviour of Mr Vorguilla. As if he had to show me a decent courtesy in the presence of his friend. It could also have been that he sensed a change in me. People do sense the difference, when you are not afraid of them any more. He would not be sure of this difference and he would have no idea how it came about, but it would puzzle him and make him more careful. He agreed with Leslie when Leslie said I was well out of that job and he even went on to say that the woman sounded like the sort of hard-bitten chiseller you sometimes found in that kind of hole-in-corner establishment in Toronto.

'And she had no business not paying you,' he said.

'You'd think the husband might have come forward,' said Leslie. 'If he was the druggist, he was the boss.'

'He ought to brew up a special dose,' Mr Vorguilla said. 'For his wife.'

It wasn't so hard to pour out tea and offer milk and sugar and pass sandwiches, and even talk, when you knew something other people didn't know, about a danger they were in. It was just because he didn't know, that I could feel something other than loathing for Mr Vorguilla. It wasn't that he had changed in himself – or if he had changed it was probably because I had. I had changed enough to feel now almost less uneasy with him than I would have to feel with Queenie.

Mr Vorguilla soon said that it was time for him to go to work. He went to change his clothes. Then Leslie asked me if I would like to have supper with him.

'Just around the corner there's a place I go,' he said. 'Nothing fancy. Nothing like Stan's place.'

I was glad enough to hear that it wouldn't be any place fancy. I said, 'Sure.' And after we had dropped off Mr Vorguilla at the restaurant we drove in Leslie's car to a fish and chips place. Leslie ordered the Super Dinner – though he had just consumed several chicken sandwiches – and I ordered the Regular. He had a beer and I had a Coke.

He talked about himself. He said he wished he had gone to Teachers' College himself instead of choosing music which did not make for a very settled life.

I was too absorbed in my own situation even to ask him what kind of musician he was. My father had bought me a return ticket, saying, 'You never know how things are going to sit with him and her.' I had thought of that ticket at the moment I watched Queenie tucking Andrew's letter under the fold of her underpants. Even though I didn't yet know that it was Andrew's letter.

I hadn't just come to Toronto, or come to Toronto to get a summer job. I had come to be part of Queenie's life, or if necessary, part of

Queenie's and Mr Vorguilla's life. Even when I had the fantasy about Queenie living with me, the fantasy had something to do with Mr Vorguilla and how she would be serving him right.

And when I'd thought of the return ticket I was taking something else for granted. That I could go back and live with Bet and my father and be part of their life.

My father and Bet. Mr and Mrs Vorguilla. Queenie and Mr Vorguilla. Even Queenie and Andrew. These were couples and each of them, however disjointed, had now or in memory a private burrow with its own heat and confusion, from which I was cut off. And I had to be, I wished to be, cut off, for there was nothing I could see in their lives to instruct me or encourage me.

Leslie too was a person cut off. Yet he talked to me about various people he was connected to by ties of blood or friendship. His sister and her husband. His nieces and nephews, the married couples he visited and spent holidays with. There was not one of these people he did not see in a fairly sunny light. All had problems but all had value. He talked about their jobs, lack of jobs, talents, strokes of luck, errors in judgment, with great interest but a lack of passion. He was cut off, or so he appeared to be, from love or vengefulness.

I would have seen flaws in this, later in my life. I would have felt the impatience, even suspicion, a woman can feel towards a man who lacks a motive. Who has only friendship to offer and offers that so easily and bountifully that even if it is rejected he can move along as buoyantly as ever. Here was no solitary fellow hoping to hook up with a girl. Even I could see that, inexperienced as I was. Just a person who took comfort in the moment and in a sort of reasonable façade of life.

His company was just what I needed at the moment, though I hardly realised it. Probably he was being deliberately kind to me. As I had thought of myself being kind to Mr Vorguilla, or at least protecting him, so unexpectedly, a little while before.

★

I was at Teachers' College when Queenie ran away again. I got the news in a letter from my father. He said that he did not know just how or when it happened. Mr Vorguilla hadn't let him know for a while, and then he had, in case Queenie had come back home. My father had told Mr Vorguilla he didn't think there was much chance of that. In the letter to me he said that at least it wasn't now the kind of thing we would say Queenie wouldn't do.

For years, even after I was married, I would get a Christmas card from Mr Vorguilla. Sleighs laden with bright parcels; a happy family in a decorated doorway, welcoming friends. Perhaps he thought these were the sort of scenes that would appeal to me, in my present way of life. Or perhaps he picked them blindly off the rack. He always included a return address, reminding me of his existence and letting me know where he was, in case of any news.

I had given up expecting that kind of news. I never even found out if it was Andrew Queenie went away with, or somebody else. Or whether she stayed with Andrew, if he was the one. When my father died there was some money left, and a serious attempt was made to trace her, but without success.

But now something has happened. Now in the years when my children are grown up and my husband has retired, and he and I are travelling a lot, I have an idea that sometimes I see Queenie. It's not through any particular wish or effort that I see her, and it's not as if I believed it was really her, either.

Once it was in a crowded airport, and she was wearing a sarong and a flower-trimmed straw hat. Tanned and excited, rich-looking, surrounded by friends. And once she was among the women at a church door waiting for a glimpse of the wedding party. She wore a spotty suede jacket that time, and she did not look either prosperous or well. Another time she was stopped at a crosswalk, leading a string of nursery-school children on their way to the swimming-pool or the park. It was a hot day and her thick middle-aged figure was frankly and comfortably on view, in flowered shorts and a sloganed T-shirt.

The last and the strangest time was in a supermarket in Twin Falls, Idaho. I came around a corner carrying the few things I had collected for a picnic lunch, and there was an old woman leaning on her shopping-cart, as if waiting for me. A little wrinkled woman with a crooked mouth and an unhealthy-looking brownish skin. Hair in yellow-brown bristles, purple pants hitched up over the small mound of her stomach – she was one of those thin women who have nevertheless, with age, lost the convenience of a waistline. The pants could have come from some thrift shop and so could the gaily coloured but matted and shrunken sweater buttoned over a chest no bigger than a ten-year-old's.

The shopping-cart was empty. She was not even carrying a purse.

Unlike those other women, this one seemed to know that she was Queenie. She smiled at me with such merriment of recognition, and such a yearning to be recognised in return, that you would think this was a moment granted to her when she was let out of the shadows for one day in a thousand.

And all I did was stretch my mouth at her, as at a loony stranger, and keep on going towards the check-out.

Then in the parking lot I made an excuse to my husband, said I'd forgotten something, and hurried back into the store. I went up and down the aisles, looking. And in just that little time the old woman seemed to have gone. She might have gone out right after I did, and be making her way now along the streets of Twin Falls. On foot, or in a car driven by some relative or neighbour, or even in a car she drove herself. They must have turned up the air-conditioning – it was so cold in there I felt as if I was breathing ice. I felt my loss.